A *Little, Brown* Book

First published in Great Britain in 1992
by Little, Brown and Company

A CIP catalogue record for this book is available from
the British Library.

ISBN 0 316 90392 2

Printed and bound in Italy by Graphicom SRL.

Little, Brown and Company (UK) Limited
165 Great Dover Street
London SE1 4YA

Clangers

The Hoopicopter

STORY BY OLIVER POSTGATE
PICTURES BY PETER FIRMIN

LITTLE, BROWN AND COMPANY

Tiny Clanger was upset. She sat on a lump of moon-rock and gazed glumly into the dark sky. All the other Clangers had gone indoors to have green soup but she had felt too miserable to eat. So she had stayed outside and was sitting staring at something that looked like a rather untidy star.

In fact it was a rather untidy star. It was the nest of the Iron Chicken, a floating heap of pieces of old iron, plastic and electronic equipment that had been lost by various spacecraft as they zoomed about. The Iron Chicken had gathered them together to make her nest.

Tiny Clanger was unhappy because she wanted to go and see her new friend the Iron Chicken.

She had looked at the Iron Chicken's nest through Major Clanger's telescope and she had seen her sitting on it, so large and clear that Tiny had called out to her. But the Iron Chicken hadn't taken any notice. This puzzled Tiny Clanger because she knew that the Iron Chicken would have been pleased to hear from her. Then, when Tiny took her eye away from the telescope she saw that the nest was really a long, long way away, far too far for her friend to hear her calling, and that made her feel miserable as well as puzzled.

Tiny Clanger was even more miserable because she had found a purple jewel-berry and she wanted to give it to the Iron Chicken as a present. It was a particularly beautiful jewel-berry which shone with purple lights that seemed to come from deep inside it. Tiny Clanger thought it would look very beautiful on the gold chain that she had given her friend.

Tiny sniffed and walked away. She sat beside the music trees and shed a tear.

The music trees were sorry to see her so sad. They played a very soft tune for her.

"I wish I knew some way to fly to the Iron Chicken's nest," said Tiny Clanger to the music trees. "I wish *you* knew a way I could fly there, but I know you don't. You music trees are not really *useful* at all. All you can do is make music!"

That was rather a rude thing to say to the music trees but they did not mind because they could see that Tiny Clanger was feeling very unhappy. Also it wasn't true. They *did* know a way that Tiny Clanger could fly to see her friend and they shook their branches so that a set of notes fell . . . *plong, plung, plang, pling* . . . on to the ground at her feet.

Tiny Clanger picked up the notes. "Thankyou music trees!" she said, feeling rather puzzled.

The music trees trilled with pleasure. They were as happy as harps because they had been able to help Tiny Clanger.

Unfortunately Tiny Clanger had no idea how to use the music notes to help her fly. She held them in her hand and looked at them and wondered. Then, suddenly, because she was really a very clever Clanger, an idea came to her.

She squeaked and ran to find a good strong hoop from the hoop-tree. She took a tiny wheel from a wheel-tree and fixed the notes around the edge of it so that they stuck out like spokes. Then she found a big nail and fixed the wheel of notes to the top of the hoop.

She turned the wheel of notes and as they turned they played a rising scale. A rising scale is a tune in which each note is a bit higher than the one before. As the rising scale was played, Tiny saw that the whole hoop began to rise as well.

"A musical hoopicopter!" shouted Tiny Clanger.

Without wasting a moment she picked up the jewel-berry and sat her fat little body in the hoop. "And up we go!" she shouted and span the wheel as hard as she could . . .

Plong, plung, plang, pling,
    Plong, plung, plang, pling,
        Plong, plung, plang, pling . . .

The notes played and as they played the hoopicopter rose swiftly into the sky, riding up on the rising scale of music. Tiny shifted her weight so that it headed towards the Iron Chicken's nest, and away they went.

Small Clanger had come outside especially to find Tiny Clanger and ask her to come into the living-cave and have some soup. When he saw the hoopicopter shooting away into the depths of space, he hooted with alarm.

Major Clanger came running out. He ran to his telescope and turned it towards the hoopicopter. He hoped he would be able to see that Tiny's unusual flying machine was carrying her well, but what he saw made him very frightened.

"The thing!" he shouted. "The thing she is flying on is breaking up! I must rescue her! Help me set up the big rocket!"

While Small Clanger ran to help his father set up the big rocket, Mother Clanger watched Tiny Clanger through the telescope. She saw that the notes had come adrift from the wheel, that the wheel had jammed and wouldn't turn and that everything was just floating loose in space. Tiny was not in any real danger, just floating there, but she was a very long way away, all alone in space.

"Five . . . four . . . three . . . two . . . one . . . zero." *WHOOOOOSH!*

Away went the big double-barrelled rocket with the little cabin. It was the biggest and most powerful rocket the Clangers had, but unfortunately the little cabin with Major Clanger sitting in it had not been fixed on very well. It was left behind on the ground as the rockets streaked away.

"Oh, what shall we do? What shall we do?" wailed Grannie Clanger.

Mother Clanger was watching through the telescope. "The Iron Chicken has spotted her!" she shouted. "She is flying down to rescue her."

Tiny Clanger was very pleased to see her friend come swooping down from the sky. The Iron Chicken picked her up quite gently and lifted her to her untidy nest. So Tiny had arrived quite safely after all.

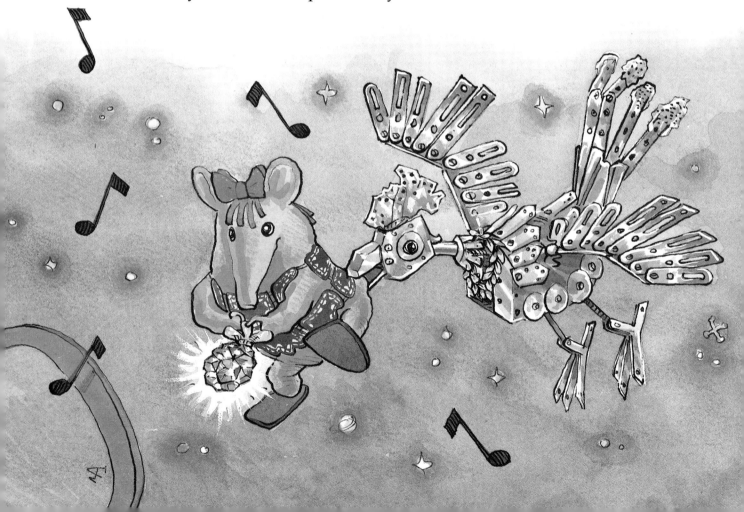

"We must rescue her!" cried Major Clanger. "We must fetch her back! Tiny is a very naughty Clanger. She should not have gone flying without asking us first!"

"She seems to be enjoying herself," said Small Clanger who was watching through the telescope.

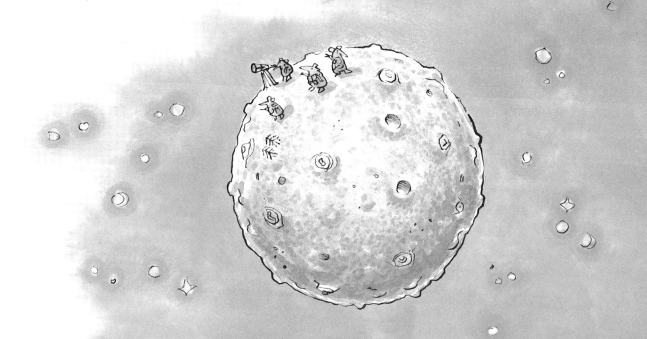

Tiny Clanger certainly was enjoying herself. She had given the jewel-berry to the Iron Chicken, who was quite delighted with it and now the two of them were sitting, having a cup of whatever it is iron chickens have for tea and chatting about whatever Clangers and iron chickens chat about. She was in no hurry to go home.

But Mother Clanger was worried. "Tiny can't stay out there on that untidy nest," she said. "There is no green soup and no blue-string pudding out there. We must find a way to bring her back!"

The trouble was that none of the Clangers could think of a way to bring Tiny Clanger back. The only rockets they had left were small ones, not powerful enough to reach the nest.

Small Clanger walked over to the music trees and sat beside them.

"You thought of a way to fly Tiny away," he said. "Now think of a way to bring her back."

The music trees played a short tune and, as if it had been called, the cloud floated over and hovered above them.

"Will the cloud help us?" asked Small.

The music trees rang like bells.

Small Clanger looked at the cloud and wondered how it would be able to help fetch Tiny Clanger. Then, suddenly, because he was really a very clever Clanger, an idea came to him.

"We will blow it!" he shouted.

From then on it was fairly easy to organise. Small Clanger called out all the Clangers and stood them in a line along the ground, a line which pointed towards the Iron Chicken's nest.

Then the cloud floated over the first Clanger in the line.

"Blow!" shouted Small Clanger.

The first Clanger, who was Uncle Clanger, blew as hard as he could through his long pointed nose.

"*Pufff!*"

The cloud began to move. As it passed over the next Clanger in the line, Grannie Clanger, Small shouted "Blow!" And Grannie Clanger blew.

"*Pufff!*"

As the cloud passed over each Clanger in the line, it was blown along with a powerful puff and by the time it passed over the last Clanger it was travelling really fast, heading like a soft spaceship towards the Iron Chicken's nest.

Tiny Clanger was really very pleased to see the cloud appear. To tell the truth she had begun to wonder how she was going to go home.

She said a fond farewell to the Iron Chicken and stepped on to the cloud.

With a few beats of her strong wings the Iron Chicken set up a space-wind that blew the cloud swiftly back the way it had come.

"Here I am!" shouted Tiny Clanger happily.

Of course her mother and father and all the other Clangers were very glad to see Tiny come back safe and sound, but they were very angry with her for flying away without asking. They were so angry that they wouldn't even let her tell them about the little silver hat with a blue light on the top that the Iron Chicken had given her as a present. They sent her straight to her bed-cave and slammed the lid down.

Before she curled up to sleep, Tiny Clanger pressed a button on her silver hat. *Beep-beep*, it went. As you have probably guessed, the silver hat was a tiny two-way radio. Tiny Clanger was now able to talk to her friend whenever she wanted to.

"Goodnight Iron Chicken," said Tiny Clanger. "Thankyou for a lovely tea party, and thankyou for the hat. You do give really *useful* presents!"

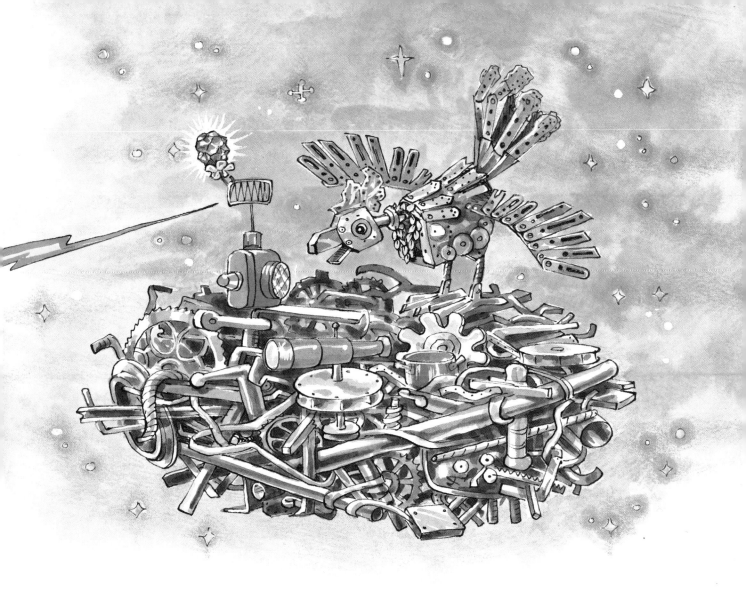

"Goodnight Tiny Clanger," came the voice of the Iron
Chicken. "Sleep well!"